TONY BALONEY

Pen Pal

BY
PAM MUÑOZ RYAN

ILLUSTRATED BY
EDWIN FOTHERINGHAM

SCHOLASTIC PRESS · NEW YORK

To Phil and Cassie Masterson, our pals —P.M.R.

To my family —E.F.

Text copyright © 2014 by Pam Muñoz Ryan
Illustrations copyright © 2014 by Edwin Fotheringham

Library of Congress Cataloging-in-Publication Data Available

ISBN 978-0-545-69227-4
12 11 10 9 8 7 6 5 4 3 2 1   14 15 16 17 18 19
Printed in the U.S.A.   40
This edition first printing, January 2014

The text in this book was set in Adobe Caslon Pro Regular.
The display type was set in P22 Kane. The title was hand lettered by Edwin Fotheringham.
The illustrations were created using digital media.
Book design by Marijka Kostiw

CONTENTS

PEN PAL MONTH

Tony Baloney,

the macaroni penguin,

hurries to the bus stop.

Today kicks off

Pen Pal Month at school!

"Every year my pen pal
is a friend for life,"
Big Sister Baloney
tells her seatmate.

Tony Baloney hopes

his pen pal will be a

friend for life too.

You

WRITE TO

I'LL 🐦 ME

WRITE TO

You Write To Unite

REACH

OUT WITH

WORDS

In class, Mrs. Gamboney beams.

"Our pen pal letters are here!

We will write back and forth

all month. Then we will meet

and have a pizza party."

8

HOMEWORK
Write letters to your pen pals
1. Tell about your family and pets.
2. Tell what you like and don't like.
3. Ask questions.
4. Use best handwriting.
5. Do slow and careful work!

Everyone cheers!

After school,

Momma and Poppa Baloney

ask about the pen pals.

Big Sister Baloney says,

"My pen pal is Irene.

She plays the violin.

She is a star student.

She is a big sister too.

We are a perfect match."

Tony Baloney says,

"My pen pal is Sam.

He rides a scooter.

He plays baseball.

He is in the middle

of his family like me.

We are a perfect match too."

Tony Baloney works hard

on his letter to Sam.

It takes forever,

or maybe one hour.

Dear Sam,
~~Thanks~~ Thanks for your letter.
I like baseball and scooters too.
I have a big sister who
never
is ~~sometimes or maybe always~~
~~bossy~~ I have baby sisters
who are bothersome. I wish
some
I had a pet, but I dont.
I have a stuffed animal buddy.
His name is Dandelion. What
about you? Your pen pal, Tony Baloney

P.S. I do not like mushrooms

Then Big Sister Baloney

corrects his spelling.

Tony Baloney does not love trouble . . .

. . . but trouble loves him.

13

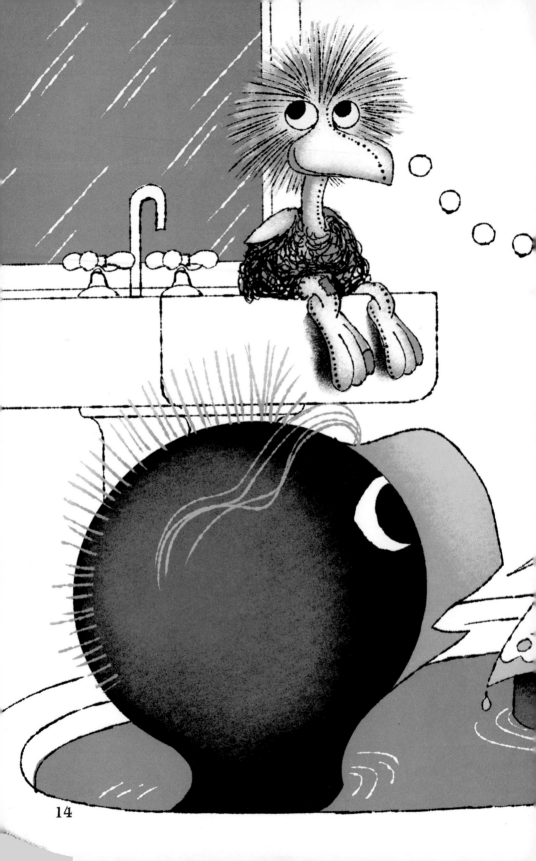

14

Tony Baloney calms down in a warm bath.

Momma says that Big Sister was only trying to help, and that my letter is fine just the way it is.

Breathe in, breathe out.

Do you think Sam will mind my messy handwriting?

A true friend won't mind.

I forgot to ask him if he has a best stuffed animal buddy.

Ask him and I'll dream the dream!

Dear Tony,

My name is Sam. I go to Patagonia Elementary hool. I love to ters and play e you wil Bes

A PERFECT MATCH

Tony Baloney and Sam
write back and forth.
They have *a lot* in common.
They both like
reading spooky stories.
They both like camping.
They both like riding *fast*
on their scooters.

At school, Tony Baloney tells Bob,
"Sam sent me a knock-knock joke
that was *so* funny. Want to hear it?"
"Not again," says Bob.
"I'm reading a letter
from *my* pen pal."

Tony Baloney tells Mrs. Gamboney,
"Sam has a stuffed animal
buddy like me. It's a tiger named Tiger."
"Yes," says Mrs. Gamboney,
"you told me twice,
or maybe every day, this week."

At home, Tony Baloney

asks Momma Baloney,

"Can Sam go on vacation with us?"

"Let's meet Sam first, shall we?"

says Momma Baloney.

At last it is the day

of the pizza party.

"I can't wait to meet Irene,"

says Big Sister Baloney.

"She is going to love me."

"Sam is the long-lost brother
I've always wanted!"
says Tony Baloney.
"Today will be the
best day of my life."

PIZZA PARTY

Mrs. Gamboney's class
prepares for the party.

How to Treat Guests

1. Welcome them.

2. Show them around.

3. Make them comfy.

4. Use best manners.

WELCOME

They make name tags.

They decorate.

They talk about manners.

Mrs. Gamboney says,

"Even if your pen pal

is not what you expect,

be kind and thoughtful."

Finally, the pen pals arrive.

Tony Baloney looks for Sam.

But he does not

see him anywhere.

Did he miss the bus?

Did he stay home?

Tony Baloney's heart sinks.

All of the pen pals pair up,

except for Tony Baloney.

He hugs Dandelion.

Then he hears someone say,

"Where is Tony Baloney?"

It is Sam.

But Sam is not

the long-lost brother

Tony Baloney always wanted.

Sam is not

a perfect match.

Sam is a *girl*.

Tony Baloney forgets all about

being kind and thoughtful.

He runs out of the room.

Mrs. Gamboney follows him.

Tony Baloney and Mrs. Gamboney have a one-on-one talk.

Mrs. Gamboney said she knows I'm a little, or maybe a lot, disappointed, but a friend is a friend, no matter what. And she's *sure* I can be polite for just one day.

Can you?

I suppose. But this is definitely *not* the best day of my life.

At least there is pizza.

30

A FRIEND
IS A FRIEND

Back inside, Tony Baloney hands

Sam her name tag.

"Sam is short for Samantha," she says.

"Yeah, I figured," says Tony Baloney.

He remembers his manners.

"Want some pizza?" he asks.

Sam smiles. "Hold the mushrooms."

The pen pals
stay all day.

They play baseball.
Sam hits a home run.

They race scooters

at recess—*fast*.

They read spooky stories.

35

At the end of the day,

everyone says good-bye.

Tony Baloney tells Sam,

"I hope you come back sometime."

And he means it.

"Your class is visiting ours

next month," says Sam.

"See you then, Tony Baloney!"

Back home, Poppa Baloney
asks about the party.
"Irene was sort of bossy,"
says Big Sister Baloney.

"Sam is a girl,"

says Tony Baloney.

"What a day of surprises!"

says Momma Baloney.